PETOOK

An Easter Story

PETOOK
An Easter Story

BY

Caryll Houselander

ILLUSTRATED BY

Tomie dePaola

Holiday House/New York

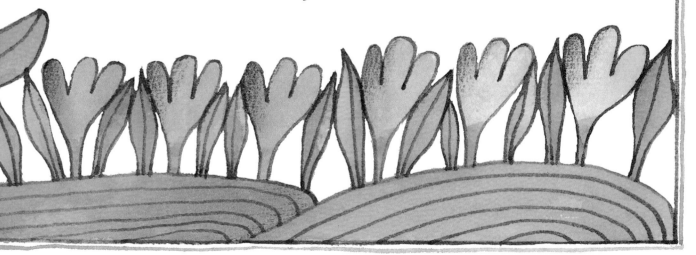

Library of Congress Cataloging-in-Publication Data

Houselander, Caryll.
Petook : An Easter story.

Summary: Petook the rooster witnesses the
crucifixion of Christ and rejoices in the birth of
new chicks three days later on Easter morning.
[1. Easter—Fiction.   2. Chicken—Fiction]
I. De Paola, Tomie, ill.   II. Title
PZ7.H8165Pe   1988   [E]   87-21228
ISBN 0-8234-0681-4

For Mother Placid, O.S.B.,
who knows about Easter

It was a lovely warm day. The sky was bright blue and the clouds white and thick, like balls of cotton wool. Everything seemed full of color, big happy colors like those in a painting book. Even the maize in the bowls was yellower than usual.

Petook was happy. He had reason to be: he was a fine cock with snowy white plumage and a red comb that positively glowed in the sun, and today he had become the father of twelve little chickens.

He thought that there were no chickens like them, none so round, so yellow, so fluffy, so bright-eyed. As for his wife Martha, the brown speckled hen, plain and homely soul though she was, she had become all grand and important.

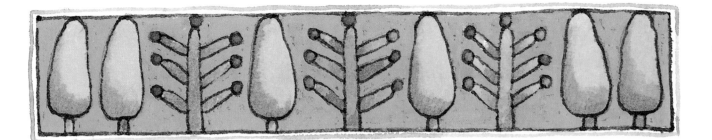

During the past weeks Petook had sometimes felt a little impatient. It seemed that Martha had some secret that he did not share. It made *her* very happy, but it also made her look almost *smug,* and it annoyed Petook to be outside of it. Martha had just sat on the eggs with a tiny smile on her face and her eyes nearly shut, as if she were looking into herself at a ball of light that was growing inside. Not talking, not moving, only making a funny little sound of happiness in her throat now and then. But now Petook understood. It was he who was smiling, and so bursting with pride and joy that he could not speak.

Petook was sitting on the wooden gatepost dreaming of his family when a group of hens ran up to him. "Come!" they clucked, "some stranger has been walking through the vineyard." Petook, who was as inquisitive as any hen, though he would not have liked it to be known, got up at once and hurried off with the others.

Sure enough, there on the dewy grass beneath the vines were the impressions of a child's feet. They were set in a straight line toward Jerusalem. But Petook knew that between the vine and the road to Jerusalem was the chicken run, and Martha and the children. He began to fly, in short violent bursts of flight, back to his family.

All the way he was saying to himself, "I am sure that they were a boy's footsteps and boys are sometimes careless, even when they're not cruel. He might tread on one of the chicks." Petook could see that some of the fruit fallen under the vines *had* been trodden and crushed.

When he got to Martha he knew that he need not have been afraid. It is true that there was a boy there, but this boy was kneeling by the little brown hen with a look of wonder on his face, quite spellbound by the lovely sight of Martha gathering the chicks under her wings.

His hands, which were thin and golden colored, were spread out like protecting wings over Martha. His lips were slightly parted, his eyes shining. So rapt was he that Petook thought, "It must be the first time that he has seen a hen gathering her chickens." For Martha, prouder than ever, was clucking softly and pushing the little ones in under her wings.

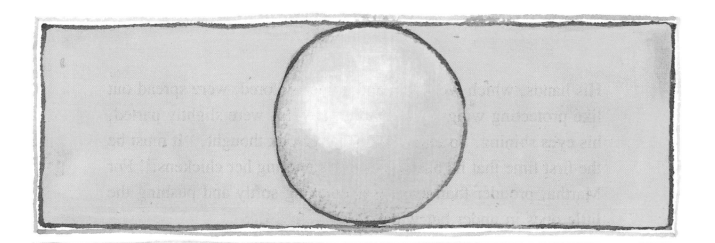

Petook preened himself. He strutted up and down, and round and round. He noticed every detail of the day, just as people notice every detail in a picture if it is rare and lovely, and one which they may not see again. He noticed how strong-looking the slim hands were, that the child's garment was woven without a seam, and that the sandaled feet were stained with the splashes of juice by treading on fruit fallen from the vine. Suddenly, for sheer joy, Petook lifted his head and crowed.

Years had gone by. Petook was quite old. He had just passed through an uneasy night. Everything had been steeped in moonlight, but all had looked strange and sad. He could see the distant hill of Calvary where the three tall trunks always stood. Only when someone was to die did the trunks become crosses, for then the poor person brought the beam that was fastened across the trunks for him to hang on. By getting on top of the dovecot and stretching his neck, Petook could just see the trunks as dark bars on the shining sky.

It seemed as if morning would never come. Martha was puffed out, sleeping on her eggs and there was no one to talk to. The moonlight made long black shadows on the grass, and the grass was like pale green water.

But suddenly there came a break in the sky and like a red wound
morning came. And suddenly Petook crowed out loud and long,
for he felt somehow excited and lifted up, he could not tell why.

All day long he kept returning to the dovecot and looking, as if a spell were on him, at the trunks. At about midday, or maybe a little after, Petook saw that there was a little smudge at the top of the hill, which must be people. And then the cross beam went up. When he saw it he slowly opened his wings, for to him the cross looked just like that, like the opening of great wings.

Of course, he did not know who was being lifted up there. He did not know that it was the lovely little boy, or that the little boy had remembered Martha and her chicks years after, and had said to hardhearted men: ''Jerusalem, Jerusalem, how often would I have gathered you under my wings as the hen gathers her chicks, and you would not.''

It was three days later, a morning cloaked with sunlight as with a garment of golden gossamer. Petook's dark mood had changed. He had a feeling of certainty that Martha's chicks would come out of the eggs today. It would be dawn in a few minutes, and the chicks would come. He felt sure of it.

There was a soft step on the grass. It was the farmer's wife. She loved the fowls, and they trusted her. Now she knelt down by Martha, and Martha did not open her eyes, but made a soft gurgle of greeting in her throat. The woman put her hand gently under the hen's breast and drew out an egg.

It was a lovely egg, a soft golden pink color, and it lay in the palm of the kind hand, warm and beautiful. The woman put the egg back, then she leaned down; she was listening. Petook was listening too.

So were the blades of grass, and the drops of dew on them, so were the leaves on the trees, and the stars that lingered still in the sky. The world was listening. Petook knew that. The trees everywhere were listening. All the winds held their breath. Every flower and leaf and bird was still. It was so quiet that Petook heard the chickens in the eggs tapping softly with their beaks to get out.

Yes, Petook heard that, and he heard life everywhere, tapping softly, knocking softly to get out, to come out of the dark into the light, out of silence into sound, out of death into life: bird and beast and seed in the earth and bud on the tree. Petook heard all that when the chickens tapped to get out.

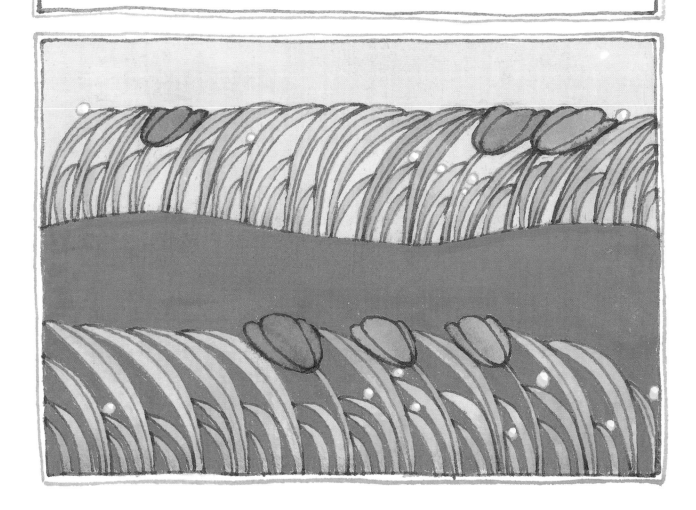

And suddenly one of them came, a struggling splutter of gold fluff. The woman laughed, and the sky broke into a splendor of light.

Petook threw back his head and crowed and crowed and crowed. His red comb burned in glory, the white feathers in his plumage dazzled in the light, the new chicken danced at his feet. He crowed again and again and again.

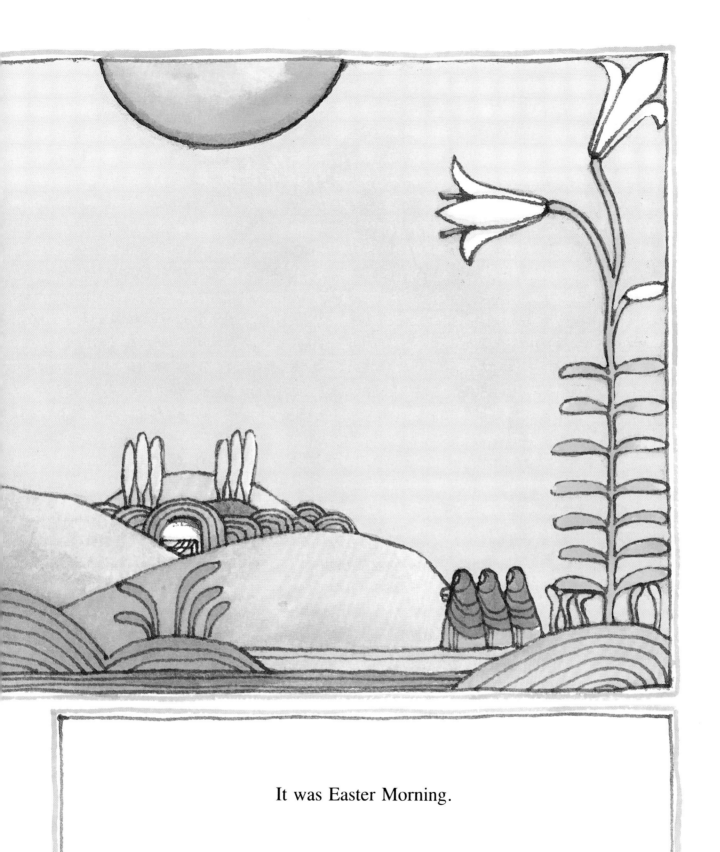

It was Easter Morning.

CARYLL HOUSELANDER was a remarkable woman. An artist, a mystic, a counselor, a great spiritual writer, she was endowed with extra-sensory perception and was, by her own admission, a neurotic. However, this Englishwoman, born in 1901 and having suffered through two world wars, stated over and over again in her writings for adults that even neurosis could be a path to sainthood—if an unwavering and complete faith in God were present.

I was introduced to the writings of Houselander in 1955 by my dear friend Mother Placid, a Benedictine nun at Regina Laudis Abbey in Bethlehem, Connecticut. Needless to say, I was delighted to find that Caryll Houselander devoted much of her time and talents to the service of children, since that focus was also a conscious choice of mine.

Many years have passed since I read my first Houselander book, and once more Holiday House and my editor Margery Cuyler have helped me to realize a "dream"—to someday illustrate one of Caryll Houselander's stories for children.

We chose "Petook" because of its Easter message of birth, rebirth, and resurrection. Petook's joy at the emergence of new life from the egg certainly echoes the joy of Christ's emergence from the tomb. It also breathes new life into the age-old symbol of the Easter egg, helping the reader become aware that it is more than just the tasty chocolate treat that we associate with Easter today. Without symbols such as this, Christianity becomes pale.

TOMIE dePAOLA
August 15, 1987